Based on the novels by Nancy Spr

Enola HOLMES

The Graphic Novels

Book One

Serena Blasco

Translated by Tanya Gold

Andrews McMeel
PUBLISHING®

I'd like to thank my family for their support and for being my first fans.

I'd also like to thank everyone at and around Gottferdom Studio for their advice and support. I would list everyone's name here, but that would make this a very long dedication. (It's like clothing tags. They end up getting in the way and you have to cut them off!)

Thanks also to all my friends who have joined me on this journey!

Serena Blasco

Enola Holmes: The Graphic Novels (Book 1) copyright © 2022 by Serena Blasco. Translated by Tanya Gold. All rights reserved. Printed in China. No part of this book may be used or reproduced in any manner whatsoever without written permission except in the case of reprints in the context of reviews.

Andrews McMeel Publishing
a division of Andrews McMeel Universal
1130 Walnut Street, Kansas City, Missouri 64106
www.andrewsmcmeel.com

Adapted from the series of novels entitled "The Enola Holmes Mysteries,"
written by Nancy Springer and first published by Philomel Books
(The Penguin Group, New York, USA) and by éditions Nathan in French

Volume 1
Copyright © 2006 by Nancy Springer
Graphic adaptation © Jungle! 2015,
by Serena Blasco

Volume 2
Copyright © 2007 by Nancy Springer
Graphic adaptation © Jungle! 2016,
by Serena Blasco

Volume 3
Copyright © 2008 by Nancy Springer
Graphic adaptation © Jungle! 2016,
by Serena Blasco

22 23 24 25 26 SDB 10 9 8 7 6 5 4 3 2 1
ISBN: 978-1-5248-7132-1
Library of Congress Control Number: 2021948436

Made by:
King Yip (Dongguan) Printing & Packaging Factory Ltd.
Address and location of production:
Daning Administrative District, Humen Town
Dongguan Guangdong, China 523930
1st Printing — 2/7/22

ATTENTION: SCHOOLS AND BUSINESSES

Andrews McMeel books are available at quantity discounts with bulk purchase
for educational, business, or sales promotional use. For information, please e-mail
the Andrews McMeel Publishing Special Sales Department:
specialsales@amuniversal.com.

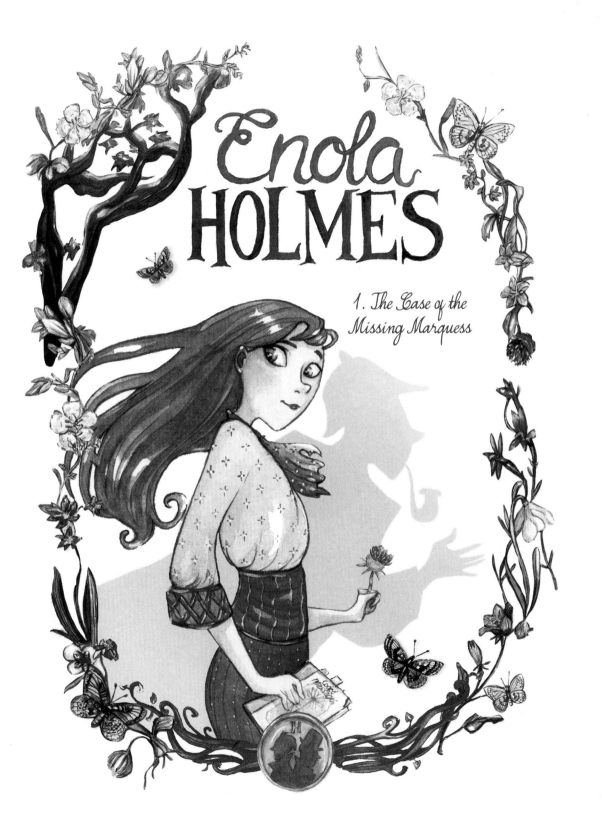

Enola
HOLMES

1. The Case of the
Missing Marquess

2

She still wasn't home in the morning. And she hadn't sent any news.

This was unusual. Some days she left with her watercolors tucked under her arm and didn't return until dinnertime.

But she always found a way of letting us know she'd be late.

There was no way I was going to just wait around and worry!

If that day were any normal day, I would have been climbing trees and looking for new hiding spots.

But that was not a day for play.

I went down every road and checked all of Mum's favorite spots.

Every time I didn't find her, I became more and more concerned.

Still nothing. What if she were hurt, unable to move or call out, or worse? Or what if she . . .

No. What a terrible thought.

I kept going until I reached the village. She sometimes spent the night there when it was too late to travel home.

3

4

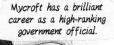

*Activists fighting for women's right to vote

Well, either she has terrible habits, or she left in a hurry.

She is 64, after all.

?!!

Thistles and sweet peas? How odd.

Your mother was quite odd.

She still is, Sherlock.

Of course.

So, what are your theories? Take out your magnifying glass. Use your skills!

There are no more clues here.

The garden then?

Not after a day of rain. Wherever she went, she is being completely reckless!

*British writer and a pioneer of the feminist movement who wrote progressive family sagas.

A book on the language of flowers, a box of watercolors, and a hand-bound notebook full of coded messages!

Alone = Enola

It is backwards!

Oh, my. That first one looks like gibberish!

ENOLA LOOK IN MY CHRYSANTHEMUMS

I'm going to copy it and remove the spaces. They are probably there to make things seem more complicated.

In her chrysanthemums?

I can't see Mum digging around the garden to hide something under some flowers.

And it's too late to go digging around the garden.

I wonder if the book on the language of flowers will help?

Chrysanthemums:

Familial attachment and affection

Attachment. That's better than nothing.

Thinking of that wilting bouquet in Mum's room, I look up "sweet pea."

Sweet Pea:
A gift upon departure! &

Thistle: Defiance.

She did leave me a message!

Right, Mum. I think I know where your chrysanthemums are.

SLAM

Sooner or later, I'll end up at a train station. I just have to avoid the ones close to Ferndell.

A Romani wagon! "Travelers," Mum called them. She let them camp on our land sometimes.

And closely followed by a peddler. Such perfect timing!

Now I'll be able to empty out all the things I have stashed in my corset and bustle.

That one is perfect!

I didn't account for rain in my infallible plan. Let's hope that doesn't happen.

Oh, look. Lights! There must be a town up ahead. It might even be big enough to have . . .

TcHHhOOOoUUUuSHhh

A train station!

Most girls who run away dress up as boys, but Sherlock would know to keep an eye out for that.

I'm going to pick something they pay much less attention to: women!

My first disguise will be . . .

Perfect. Next step: Go to London. Sherlock and Mycroft would never consider that I'd run away to end up even closer to them. London. Beautiful, brilliant London. Finally.

What should I do now?

Mrs. Holmes!

Unbelievable!

Mrs. Holmes, please forgive me for hailing you. I'm Inspector Lestrade. I know Sherlock Holmes.

Pleased to meet you.

I have to admit that Mr. Holmes never mentioned you.

And you, do you tell him about your family?

Hmm, well, no . . .

By the way, Lord Tewksbury was not kidnapped. He ran away.

What? But what about the forced door and the state of his room?

Staged. Young Tewksbury only thought of ships and wanted to run away to sea.

As well as escape an over-protective mother.

But . . .

In his crow's nest in the tree over there, there are photographs of the steamship, the Great Eastern.

You'll find him on the docks of London, ready to board.

In the tree? How did you get up there?

So much for my escape plan. Now that I've shared my real name, I'm going to need to find a new disguise quickly.

I have to admit that I very much like the idea of hiding in London right under my brothers' noses.

Are you faring well, dear?

I'm fine, thank you.

Have you been alone a long time?

No.

Just when you find a good one, he kicks the bucket.

It's always the same story.

If you ever need some extra for living expenses, take off one or two of those fine petticoats.

You won't be able to tell the difference. Sell them at a used clothing shop.

The best one is Culhane's. Easy to find. Near the docks.

Here's my card. I'll give you a good price.

Thank you.

London. Finally!

What are you doing?

ZzzZZzzzz

If I could get one of these whalebones out of my corset, I could try to cut this rope.

There we go. This is going to take a while.

Hey, you!

Stop doing that!

I said stop!

No!

I want the boat to rock!

And I said stop!

SNAP

WHACK

Oh no! What have I done!

It's fine. He's not dead. Now untie me before he wakes up!

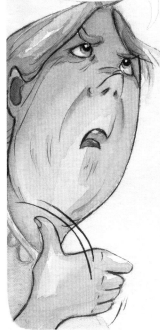

I did too! I went to ask for shoes. They laughed in my face and told me to leave.

I'm glad you want to go home. Your mother will be overjoyed.

Read all about it!

LONDON GAZETTE

Basilwether Kidnapping: Sensational Development

Ransom demand for young Viscount Tewksbury!

What?

Inspector Lestrade had thought the viscount had run away; however, an anonymous ransom demand arrived at Basilwether Hall this morning.

The spiritualist medium Madame Laelia Sibyl de Papaver senses that the viscount is being held captive . . .

The Spiritualist Medium Madame Laelia Sibyl de Papaver

. . . and declares that she is in favor of paying this ransom because not cooperating could put him in mortal danger.

Interesting!

That picture of me is terrible!

I think you need to turn yourself in to the police.

I think so too.

49

Scotland Yard, please.
It's beautiful!
Where were you hiding that notebook?
A lady never reveals her secrets.
Let's consider this again. Madame Laelia must have overheard my conversation with Inspector Lestrade.
SQUEAKY
I had told him that you were about to board the Great Eastern. Cutter found you there. And Squeaky must have followed me.
CUTTER
I think I saw Cutter on the train. Madame Laelia could have sent a telegram from Basilwether to him at the station.
And that's how Cutter found me.
But Squeaky said he recognized me. Where from?
I overheard them talking about a telegram on the boat. Maybe Madame Laelia sent them a description?
That doesn't make sense. They were discussing their messages to one another . . .

51

Scotland Yard

Even if you were the Prince of Wales, you'd still have to wait your turn!

Take a seat.

End of Episode 1

SECRET NOTEBOOK

ENOLA HOLMES

The Language of Flowers

Ivy
I will always be
faithful to you.

Thistle
I defend myself how I can.
Learn to defend yourself.

Sweet pea
A gift upon departure.

Iris
I'm sending you a message. I will
know how to prove my love.

Chamomile
Strength in adversity. I am
sincerely attached to you.

Rambling rose
Symbolizes a free and
wandering life.

Rhododendron
Something dangerous is near.
Be careful.

Violet
In all modesty.

Chrysanthemum
Familial attachment and
affection.

Primrose
May you have eternal youth.

Lily of the valley
Happiness found.

Bear's ear
Don't ask me for anything!

Mountain lettuce
I don't know how to give up.

Poppy
I'm sorry. Let me
comfort you.

Daisy
A symbol of innocence.

Narcissus
You only love yourself.
Selfish person.

Pansy
I need attention.

Blue sage
I'm thinking of you.

Saxifrage
With all my affection.

Mum's coded message:

AOEOLIMESOK
LNKONYDBBN

She bordered the message with ivy . . . Hidden meaning?

Mouse garlic, found at the cemetery.

Meaning: Fidelity

Fidelity is better than nothing . . .

ENOLA

AOEO
LNKO

My name in the first few letters! Zigzagging like ivy!

ALONEKOOLN1YMDEBSBONK

Backwards:

KNOBS | BED | MY | IN | LOOK | ENOLA

ENOLA LOOK IN MY BED KNOBS

August, 1888

THIS IS GIVING ME AN IDEA!

Closed corset

① Remove

Replace

②

Remove the padding and replace it with my belongings.

②

Do the same with the bustle. Replace the padding with a change of clothing

③

Open corset

AMPLIFIER

The Ideal Corset!

The ideal corset for thin figures. Words cannot describe the charm and grace this model will deliver. No other corset can compare!

The padded bust and hips give girls and women a well-proportioned figure with harmonious curves, a generous bust, and a narrow waist.

Satisfaction guaranteed. Beware of imitations.

Woman wearing the ideal corset

In reality, this is terrible for your body.

The corset compresses your organs and impairs breathing. You can't even sneeze!

September, 1888

KIDNAPPED HEIR!

Tewky

Article relating the facts:

Monday morning, a gardener noticed that the French doors to the billiard room had been forced open. He sounded the alarm immediately.

Thinking it was a burglary, the butler took inventory of the silver and other valuables, and found nothing was missing.

The chambermaids were the ones who discovered the scene in the room of the young viscount, only 12 years old.

The young viscount's belongings were scattered around the room, silent witnesses to a merciless struggle. The room's occupant has disappeared.

A bit melodramatic!

List written in Culhane's
- Why was Squeaky so sure I knew where Tewky was?
- What did he want with Tewky?
- Does he specialize in kidnappings?
- How did he know about the Great Eastern?

THE GREAT EASTERN

Article about the ransom demand!

Inspector Lestrade had thought the viscount had run away; however, an anonymous ransom demand arrived at Basilwether Hall this morning.

The spiritualist medium Madame Laelia Sibyl de Papaver senses that the viscount is being held captive and declares that she is in favor of paying this ransom as not cooperating could put him in mortal danger.

SQUEAKY

CUTTER

Found in the garden of Basilwether Hall. I don't know the species. Nonnative plant? Must research.

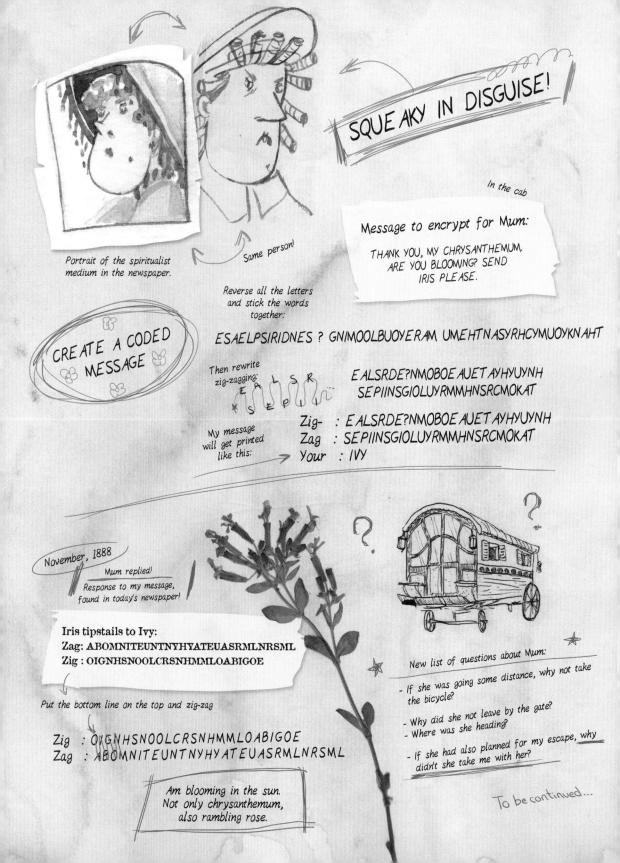

SQUEAKY IN DISGUISE!

Same person!

Portrait of the spiritualist medium in the newspaper.

In the cab

Message to encrypt for Mum:

THANK YOU, MY CHRYSANTHEMUM. ARE YOU BLOOMING? SEND IRIS PLEASE.

CREATE A CODED MESSAGE

Reverse all the letters and stick the words together:

ESAELPSIRIDNES ? GNIMOOLBUOYERAM UMEHTNASYRHCYMUOYKNAHT

Then rewrite zig-zagging:

E A L S R
E S E P I L R

E ALSRDE?NMOBOE AUET AYHYUYNH
SEPIINSGIOLUYRMMHNSRCMOKAT

My message will get printed like this:

Zig- : E ALSRDE?NMOBOE AUET AYHYUYNH
Zag : SEPIINSGIOLUYRMMHNSRCMOKAT
Your : IVY

November, 1888

Mum replied!

Response to my message, found in today's newspaper!

Iris tipstails to Ivy:
Zag: ABOMNITEUNTNYHYATEUASRMLNRSML
Zig : OIGNHSNOOLCRSNHMMLOABIGOE

Put the bottom line on the top and zig-zag

Zig : OIGNHSNOOLCRSNHMMLOABIGOE
Zag : ABOMNITEUNTNYHYATEUASRMLNRSML

Am blooming in the sun.
Not only chrysanthemum,
also rambling rose.

New list of questions about Mum:

- If she was going some distance, why not take the bicycle?

- Why did she not leave by the gate?
- Where was she heading?

- If she had also planned for my escape, why didn't she take me with her?

To be continued...

Enola
HOLMES

2. The Case of the
Left-Handed Lady

Yes. That's why I'd like to wait for Dr. Ragostin.

Dr. Watson, I'm his personal assistant. He trusts me to take down preliminary information to save him time.

It is like you do for Mr. Holmes, is it not?

That is true. However, this is a delicate matter.

And we assure complete discretion.

Mr. Holmes is currently more tormented and irritable than usual.

Since he wouldn't tell me why, I spoke to his brother, Mycroft.

How do you spell his name?

M-Y-C-R-O-F-T. It is an unusual name, much like his young sister's name, Enola.

E-N-O-L-A

Mycroft told me that their mother and sister have been missing for some months.

How terrible! Were they kidnapped?

No. they ran away. And they each left separately.

Good lord! How old is the young sister, um . . . Enola?

My lodgings are far from my offices. It is safer this way. Less expensive too.

Good evening, Mrs. Tupper.

My landlady is lovely and keeps to herself. She doesn't ask a lot of questions.

I need to figure out what to do if my brothers find me, especially since they already know about the money. They are starting to pick up on clues.

London Bridge Falling Down Urgent Must Talk

To encode the message, I break up the alphabet into five lines.

ABCDE
FGHIJ
KLMNO
PQRST
UVWXYZ

323534143534 124324142215
2444 21113232243432 14355334
514322153445 33514445 45113231

Then I replace the letters with numbers.

L: 3rd line, 2nd letter: 32
O: 3rd line, 5th letter: 35

It's time to change into my third identity.

My trusty reinforced corset, with plenty of room to stash belongings and good at deflecting knives.

And my collar to protect against cutthroats.

My nighttime life.

Sister, Sister of the Streets

Thank you, Sister. God protect you.

People? Out at this hour?

ARRGH!

Three days later

Enough self-pity. I must collect myself and get back to work.

And my first case, or Dr. Ragostin's first case, will be Lady Alistair's.

This place used to belong to none other than Madame Laelia Sibyl de Papaver, also known as Squeaky.

Who is currently rotting behind bars with his partner in crime, Cutter.

CLICK

He cleverly created secret compartments.

WHOOSH

Including a dressing room, where I could disguise myself in absolute discretion.

Identity change

To approach the Alistairs, I need to be a lady.

In future, I will never be without my dagger.

Another trick: a secret door leading out of the building.

Presenting Lady Ragostin, Dr. Ragostin's young wife.

If Cecily left of her own volition, did someone help her?

Too many questions and not enough answers.

Joddy, can you call me a carriage please? I have some errands to run.

Off to visit the presumed suitor, Alexander Finch.

The variety of products is quite impressive.

GRAND BAZAAR
FINCH & SON

Alexander! Do you call that a window display?

Luck is on my side.

Take down those anarchist colors and put up something that looks distinguished!

Yes, Sir.

Pardon me, Mr. Finch?

What can I do for you, Miss?

I seem to have gotten lost among all these wares. Could you show me . . .

Lady Theodora sent me.

Please follow me. I will show you what we have.

Here are laced boots that are in fashion.

Lady Theodora is trying to move the investigation forward on her own since the police are not making enough progress.

Indeed. But my father will not let me go anywhere where he can't keep an eye on me.

You live with your family?

No. I live above the shop with the staff. It's to punish me for "forgetting my place." I treat everyone the same and despise labels.

How did you meet Cecily?

We met in the city. She needed help with her bicycle chain.

Lady Cecily is a serious girl. She is reading Karl Marx's *Das Kapital*. And we have spoken of the exploitation of the masses.

She asked me to show her working-class life.

Is that what you wrote to one another about?

Yes.

And you brought her to the docks and working-class neighborhoods?

Precisely. She wanted her eyes opened and was asking a lot of questions:

What are pawnbrokers? What are these drippings that the poor seem so fond of?

Was she doing this for a specific reason? A project? Was she doing research?

It seems like her reason was to make me take the blame.

The blame? What for?

For running away. If a young lady runs away into the arms of a suitor, she's seen as naïve. When a lady reads Marx, she is seen as deranged and capable of anything.

Do you have any guesses as to where she might have gone?

I don't have the slightest idea. And I am stuck here.

Thank you for showing me so many styles, Mr. Finch. I will have to take some time to decide.

Dr. Watson's surgery.

Miss Meshle! To what to I owe this pleasure?

Good day, Dr. Watson.

I . . . um, Dr. Ragostin um, took a look at the case and sent me to ask you a question.

I am delighted that he is looking into the case.

He would like to know if Mr. Holmes has been looking at coded messages in the paper lately.

Mr. Holmes always reads the personal ads. They are often useful in his cases.

Yes, but coded messages?

Well, yes. But not in the papers. He's been studying a little notebook full of flowers and coded messages.

When I asked if I could see it, he slammed it shut!

Mum's notebook! He must have searched Cutter and Squeaky's boat after Tewky came back.

What's wrong, Miss Meshle? Are you unwell?

It's nothing. I have to go. Goodbye, Dr. Watson.

Back in front of the emporium

We'll see if Alexander is as much of a recluse as he claims.

Someone is leaving the staff lodgings.

SON

Alexander

How interesting. Our mysterious shop clerk is also a night owl.

You draw very well. Who are you?

And you, who are you, Lady Cecily?

What?

Do not worry. I'm only here to get you someplace warm and a good meal.

Next time, we will wave the flags of revolution.

I can't leave! I have to remain loyal!

To whom?

To Cameron Shaw. He will go down in history! Have you not heard of him?

No. But you can come with me and tell me all about him.

Had you met him before?

Never. Except in my dreams. Isn't that strange?

I have to go back.

Where? Home?

I don't have a home!

Who are you, anyway? What is your name?

Um, I . . .

Enola, Enola Holmes.

Cecily! Come here this instant!

What rotten luck. We must have walked in circles.

Who said you could leave?

111

Don't just stand there! After her!

Sound the alarm. We're looking for a man with a shoulder wound. His name is Alexander Finch. Bring me a lantern!

I need to find somewhere to hide. Sherlock is going to turn this city upside down trying to find me.

It looks like Sherlock also sleeps with his window open. Lucky for me!

I've heard that she's dressed as a nun. And she has a knife.

That girl needs to be disciplined.

SECRET NOTEBOOK

To E.H.: Come home. All will
be forgiven. No questions asked.
Please get in touch. M. & S.

To M. & S.: Rubbish! E.H.

ENOLA
HOLMES

Flower Cipher

Morning Glory: Flirtation

Rose: Passionate love

Hawthorn: Hope

Wild Rose: Poetry

Honeysuckle: Affection

Amaryllis: Pride

Wormwood: Absence

Lily of the valley: Happiness found

Forget-me-not: True love

My message:
Romani. Correct? Ivy.

I know that Mum left with the Romani. Her last message implied she was leading a free and wandering life. (Rambling rose)

My encoded message:
MY CHRYSANTHEMUM: THE THIRD LETTER OF TRUE LOVE, THE SECOND LETTER OF AFFECTION, THE FOURTH LETTER OF ABSENCE, THE FIRST LETTER OF PRIDE, THE EIGHTH LETTER OF HOPE, THE SECOND LETTER OF HAPPINESS FOUND. CORRECT? IVY.

Mum's decoded message:
Yes. Where are you, Ivy?

My reply: London

The wax seal colors have different meanings.

Lady Cecily used gray.

Red: Business correspondence

Blue: Faithful love

Gray: Friendship

Green: Encouraging a shy suitor

Purple: Condolences

Yellow: Jealousy

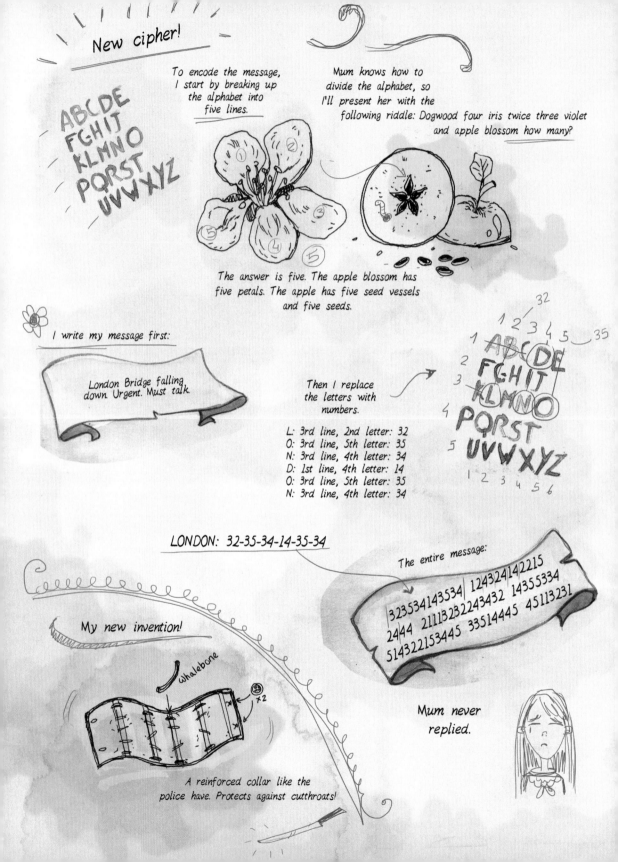

New cipher!

To encode the message, I start by breaking up the alphabet into five lines.

ABCDE
FGHIJ
KLMNO
PQRST
UVWXYZ

Mum knows how to divide the alphabet, so I'll present her with the following riddle: Dogwood four iris twice three violet and apple blossom how many?

The answer is five. The apple blossom has five petals. The apple has five seed vessels and five seeds.

I write my message first:

London Bridge falling down. Urgent. Must talk.

Then I replace the letters with numbers.

L: 3rd line, 2nd letter: 32
O: 3rd line, 5th letter: 35
N: 3rd line, 4th letter: 34
D: 1st line, 4th letter: 14
O: 3rd line, 5th letter: 35
N: 3rd line, 4th letter: 34

LONDON: 32-35-34-14-35-34

The entire message:

323534143534 | 124324142215
2444 211132322432 14355334
514322153445 33514445 45113231

My new invention!

whalebone
x2

A reinforced collar like the police have. Protects against cutthroats!

Mum never replied.

The Case of Lady Cecily

January 2

I am bored to death. Everyone is talking about new year's resolutions, but what do they matter? If only it were to make the world a better place. The streets are filled with children wearing rags and I'm being trained to walk backwards without tripping over my nine foot train. My life has no meaning, no purpose.

Cecily wrote these pages with her left hand and backwards. You can only read them in a mirror.

When father calls the poor names, I have to bite my tongue.

Being left-handed

is frowned upon. Children who tend to favor their left hand have been forced to write with their right hand. Hitting the "bad" hand with a ruler is common. Sometimes, tutors will tie a child's left hand behind their back!

Fresh Air

Apparently, sleeping with one's window open at night is healthy. It's fashionable in high society. Mum also made us sleep with the windows open.

I'm happy to do that in the country, but I don't think London air is all that healthy.

COUNTRY

LONDON

Cecily's left-handed drawing. The lines are thicker and more expressive.

Her right-handed drawing. It's hesitant and dull.

Lady Cecily also left her window open. The kidnapper could have come in through there to hypnotize her.

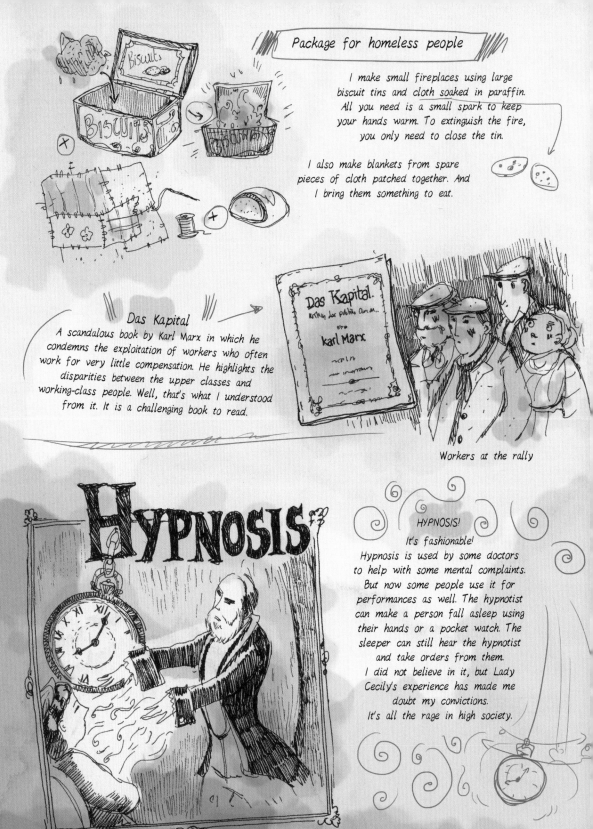

Package for homeless people

I make small fireplaces using large biscuit tins and cloth soaked in paraffin. All you need is a small spark to keep your hands warm. To extinguish the fire, you only need to close the tin.

I also make blankets from spare pieces of cloth patched together. And I bring them something to eat.

Das Kapital

A scandalous book by Karl Marx in which he condemns the exploitation of workers who often work for very little compensation. He highlights the disparities between the upper classes and working-class people. Well, that's what I understood from it. It is a challenging book to read.

Das Kapital
karl Marx

Workers at the rally

HYPNOSIS

HYPNOSIS!
It's fashionable!
Hypnosis is used by some doctors to help with some mental complaints. But now some people use it for performances as well. The hypnotist can make a person fall asleep using their hands or a pocket watch. The sleeper can still hear the hypnotist and take orders from them.
I did not believe in it, but Lady Cecily's experience has made me doubt my convictions.
It's all the rage in high society.

221 B

Sherlock's Home!
At 221B Baker Street. I found out where my brother lives and was able to dig through his belongings!

A Study in Scarlet
J. WATSON

A copy of John Watson's book, which tells the story of one of Sherlock's cases. An enthralling mystery!

Coded Messages

His violin. Sadly, I've never heard him play. Mum said he's very talented.

A chemistry set. He uses it to analyze evidence from crime scenes. He's one of few people to use science and chemistry to solve cases.

Found in a drawer: Mum's notebook, drawings of scary looking dogs, and the portrait of a woman. "I.A." is written on the back. I didn't know Sherlock had any women friends.

I.A.

His pipe. According to Watson, if a case is of average complexity, he smokes one. If it's more difficult, two. At Ferndell, when Mum disappeared, he smoked at least three.

X3!

TO IVY:

THE SECOND LETTER OF HOPE, THE SIXTH AND SEVENTH LETTERS OF PRIDE, THE FIFTH LETTER OF FLIRTATION, THE THIRD LETTER OF PASSIONATE LOVE, THE FIRST LETTER OF ABSENCE, THE FOURTH LETTER OF AFFECTION, THE THIRD LETTER OF HAPPINESS FOUND, THE THIRD LETTER OF POETRY. YOU?

YOUR CHRYSANTHEMUM.

HAWTHORN

AMARYLLIS

MORNING GLORY

ROSE

WORMWOOD

HONEYSUCKLE

LILY OF THE VALLEY

WILD ROSE

Enola
HOLMES

3. The Case of the Bizarre Bouquets

Doctor Watson is my brother Sherlock's friend. He writes books about the cases they investigate together.

FINCH

A few weeks ago, John Watson came to see me . . . well, Ivy Meshle, Dr. Ragostin's secretary . . . to try to help find me.

He unknowingly pointed me toward my first case: The case of the left-handed lady.

Wait a second.

What if this is another of Sherlock's traps? What if he's trying to draw me out?

Is that such a far-fetched idea?

It doesn't matter. Watson helped me. And he saved Lady Cecily.

If he has been kidnapped, nothing will keep me from looking for him.

Good girl.

133

DR. RAGOSTIN
PERDITORIAN
FINDER OF ALL
THINGS LOST

AWAY
ON
BUSSNESS

MILLIN

I can't risk going back.

My old office. I can't go back after Lady Cecily's case. If Watson tells Sherlock he came here, it won't be long before he connects me with this place.

And now I don't have any disguises left.

Sherlock has a better trained eye than most. I will need to disguise myself well.

I already dressed up as a nun and a hawker. He's going to expect a similar disguise.

When I was hiding at Sherlock's, I found an address for a shop selling costumes and theater props.

Chaunticleer's. And if his receipts are to be believed, he hasn't been back in five years. He goes to other shops now. In theory, I shouldn't see him there.

This must be it. I remember the rooster from the receipts.

PERTELOTE'S

It's changed names. How strange that they kept the old sign.

Hello?

There's just about every kind of accessory here. It's like a theater prop and costume shop.

How can I help you?

Mrs. Pertelote, I presume?

No. Mrs. Kippersalt.

Oh. I see that you've kept the Chaunticleer's sign.

It's an old thing. And we should take care of old things, don't you think? What are you looking for?

I was looking at this small printing kit. Do you think one could print calling cards with it?

Yes, but they wouldn't look very nice.

As you wish.

Thank you. I'm going to keep looking.

A wig made from real hair

Poor women, some of whom haven't cut their hair since they were children, sometimes sell their hair for a few coins.

Oh! Amplifiers!

To visit Mrs. Watson, I will need to look radically different.

What if I dress up like a beautiful lady?

I'm not normally one for frills, but that is perfect!

Exactly like that!

DING DONG

GENTLEMEN'S CLUB

He didn't come home that night. I called the police, but they told me it was too soon.

On Wednesday, he was out making house calls. Then he went to his club at the end of the day.

Sherlock arrived shortly after. He started investigating right away. I'm still waiting to hear from him.

Does he have any theories?

Perhaps vengeance. But since John has no enemies, he thinks someone is using my husband to get to him.

What if it's a patient?

That's possible. Mr. Holmes is looking through John's patient files. I'd rather not think of it.

You have received so many beautiful bouquets.

It's a kind gesture. I don't even know who sent them.

This one is distinctive!

Yes—strange, isn't it? White poppies instead of the usual red ones, and red hawthorn instead of the usual white. I don't even recognize those green plants.

Those are asparagus fronds.

Really? How surprising for a bouquet. How did you recognize them?

My mother was a botanist. Mrs. Watson, do you know the language of flowers?

Very little. The poppy means comfort and hawthorn means hope, right?

The red poppy does. But the white poppy symbolizes sleep.

Mind you, sleep would do me some good.

No message.

Yet there was this strange bouquet. I can't stop thinking about how malevolent it felt.

And the asparagus fronds. I don't know what they mean.

Sending a message by bouquet takes a lot of effort. Maybe it comes from someone holding an old grudge. Or someone creative. But how can I find this person?

When you send a coded message, you expect a reply, right? Someone who sends a bouquet like that expects that someone will understand its significance.

Anything is possible.

What if I put a message in the paper and pretend it's from Mary Morstan Watson?

Hawthorn, asparagus, bindweed, poppy: What do you want? Reply here. M.M.W.

That evening, back on the Watsons' street.

If this person sends another bouquet, I want to find a way of intercepting the delivery.

I put the message in a number of London papers. It should come out tomorrow.

ROOM
TO
LET

The next morning

Mrs. Tupper, I'm going to spend a few days with my aunt!

145

151

154

M M H N Y H R O E O
U E T A R C U Y V L

E W R H E T E T I E I E Y I
N H E E W O L S M R S D V

It's time to take stock.

The nose. A disguise?

What does this have to do with Dr. Watson?

The Afghan Wars? When Watson was a military doctor. An unforgiven amputation?

Mrs. Kippersalt. She practically threw me out when I brought up the nose. Does she know something?

Her husband has a hothouse.

Many Londoners have one. But it's worth checking to see if he grows white poppies and asparagus fronds.

SALLY-DOWN-THE-ALLEY

Cab!

Are you speaking to me?

The Strand please!

Can you pay for this?

If you get me there in 10 minutes, I'll even pay you double.

Very well, m'lady.

156

Who do you take me for? Do you think that I didn't see you leave as soon as my back was turned? What are you up to?

Nothing, I swear! Just taking care of my affairs.

Your affairs? All you have to do is stay home and not hurt anyone.

Hurt anyone? I need to get closer.

Nobody's hurting anymore.

And he's doing more good where he is now anyway.

Gus was right to lock you up!

And you got me out! You told them you could take care of me at home!

166

Wasn't there a woman here who didn't have a nose? I think she had a floral name. Lily? Lila?

It was Flora. A strange woman. She was here because she was dressing and acting like a man.

Why would they lock people up for that?

I heard that she only wore trousers. And she was indecent with other women, if you know what I mean.

Really?

Those are just rumors.

Mum told me about places like this, where people are locked up when they try to be different, or when they become inconvenient.

Not that we know of. Her brother-in-law had her institutionalized. It's sort of ironic. She's not here anymore and he's now one of Dr. Grey's patients.

Did she commit any crimes?

How did that happen?

Stop asking so many questions and go bring this to the nurses' room. It's on the first floor. There's a sign on the door.

Two new recruits on the same day. How unusual!

Oh no! The real new laundress just arrived.

I need to move quickly!

173

And, can you imagine, the person who solved this and helped us bring John home was Sherlock Holmes's young sister.

Sister? He has a sister?

Yes. Let's just say that she's been causing some trouble, so the family have been quiet about her. They don't even know where she is.

How intriguing!

My husband even tried to find her by going to Dr. Ragostin. He's supposed to be a specialist in missing persons.

He's surely a charlatan!

John thinks so. He never even met him, only his secretary.

DAILY TELEGRAPH

Interesting. What did Mr. Holmes think of that?

Since nothing came of it, John decided not to mention it. But he tried, at least.

Thank you again for your hospitality, Mrs. Watson. I am delighted that your husband is home and well.

End of episode 3

SECRET
NOTEBOOK

TO E.H.: COMPLIMENTS AND LAURELS.
OUR HUMBLE GRATITUDE. S.&M.

ENOLA
HOLMES

~ DR WATSON MISSING

!!!

his bag

Alarming report:

The respectable Dr. Watson, known associate of the great detective Sherlock Holmes, has mysteriously disappeared without a trace. It is possible that he was taken by one of Mr. Holmes's sworn enemies or in exchange for ransom. Another theory is that, because he is a doctor, he has been taken by an anti-vaccination group.

An investigation is in progress and his last movements are being traced.

Our thoughts are with his family and friends. If you have any information, contact the paper or the police.

221B

LIST OF QUESTIONS

- Why was Watson taken?
- A personal vengeance?
- Related to Sherlock?
- How far is Sherlock in his investigation?
- Is Mrs. Watson's mysterious bouquet linked to his disappearance?
- If it is, why send such a tortuous message and no ransom demand?

(422555) - 415144423451
334244542351545351
3532513451 35325143
23532551514354 55531534
31323455411435432513
31533

Mum's message in the paper !!!

MYCROFT

First the column, then the row

Ⅰ
1 2 3 4 5
A B C D E
F G H I J
K L M N O
P Q R S T
U V W X Y Z

Ⅱ
1
2
3
4
5

| 25   55

Decoded:

NY, DESIRE MISTLETOE. WHERE, WHEN? LOVE, YOUR CHRYSANTHEMUM

LARK LARK KRAL KRAL

A mirrored message. Mum was trying to warn me about the fake message by reminding me of illusions.

Flower Cipher

Red poppy: Comfort

White poppy: Sleep

Asparagus: ???

Laburnum: Sadness, abandonment, concealment

White hawthorn: Hope

Red hawthorn: A pagan symbol of bad luck.

Hedge bindweed: Weed, lost hope

GUS ??!

Yew springs: Funerary tree, mourning, a bad omen

Bell flower: Discouragement

Frances Kippersalt,
Proprietress of Pertelote's,
a theater-costume shop.

Her nose was eaten
by a rat when she
was a baby.

Flora Harris

Frances Kippersalt's sister. Flora never married.
Frances married Augustus Kippersalt, owner of
Chaunticleer's, which she later renamed Pertelote's.
Flora lived with the couple until she was
committed for dressing as a man.

* I still don't understand why people shouldn't wear what
they like. I would certainly feel more comfortable in
trousers. And if a man wanted to wear a dress, what
would be wrong with that?

My Disguises

The extravagant Miss Viola
Everseau. This disguise takes
the longest to put on.

Sally-down-the-alley

Miss Eudoria,
the laundress

My disguise for
escaping from Colney Hatch

221B

When I spent the night at Sherlock's, I went through his desk and cupboards. He had so many things for disguises. That's how I learned about Mrs. Kippersalt's shop.

False mustaches, scars, and warts.

So many wigs, including some that look like real hair

Face powder and false beards

And a number of other disguises

What Sherlock knows about me:
- That I disguised myself as a widow, a hawker, and a nun
- That I sometimes give food and blankets to the poor
- That I helped the police catch two criminals
- That I managed to get into his home twice
- That I use the name Ivy
- So, he might know that a woman named Ivy Meshle works for Dr. Ragostin—if Dr. Watson told him about it.

PERTELOTE'S

Pertelote's is a gold mine. You can find just about anything there. Theater costumes and all sorts of things for disguises.

The Rooster shop sign.

Amplifiers to change your body type.

Perfume and makeup.

Wigs and masks.

Ouija boards to speak to spirits and crystal balls.

BODY FOUND IN A HOTHOUSE

Flora Harris's Hothouse - 1889

Following Dr. Watson's return, the police began investigating the people responsible for his abduction, Flora Harris and Frances Kippersalt.

Overwhelming evidence was found in the hothouse behind their building.

After a meticulous search of the premises conducted by the great Sherlock Holmes, a body was found buried in a bed of asparagus.

During an interview led by Inspector Lestrade, Frances Kippersalt blamed her sister for the death of her husband, Augustus Kippersalt. Flora then admitted to the crime. She said it was because Mr. Kippersalt forced her to be committed at Colney Hatch. She also confessed to abducting Dr. Watson because he signed her committal papers.

There you have it. Flora killed Gus. Mrs. Kippersalt covered for her sister and they hid the body in a large bed of asparagus. It's the one I landed on when I fell through the roof. It saved my life.

A murder and an abduction for vengeance. Flora will surely return to Colney Hatch now. And Mrs. Kippersalt will be imprisoned for her conspiracy in her husband's murder. A sordid tale. Luckily, it ended well for Dr. Watson.

Wonderful news: Ivy Meshle will be able to return to work!

5453411155 43535343
315323435155 3211543132
114455231533 114413 125334
3334 13421414513444112354.
E.H.

A B C D E
F G H I J
K L M N O
P Q R S T
U V W X Y Z

To be continued in the next
installment of Enola Holmes:
The Graphic Novels!